KU-262-252

All children have a great ambition to read to themselves... and a sense of achievement when they can do so.

The **read it yourself** *series has been devised to satisfy their ambition. Even before children begin to learn to read formally, perhaps using a reading scheme, it is important that they have books and stories which will actively encourage the development of essential pre-reading skills. Books at Level 1 in this series have been devised with this in mind and will supplement pre-reading books available in any reading scheme.*

Based on well-known nursery rhymes and games which children will have heard, these simple pre-readers introduce key words and phrases which children will meet in later reading. Many young children will remember the words rather than read them but this is a normal part of pre-reading.

One, two, buckle my shoe *is an entertaining introduction to the number words and figures from one to twenty. In the right hand corner of each spread, there is a counting activity which encourages children to look closely at the pictures. It is recommended that the parent or teacher should read this book aloud to the child first and then go through the rhyme, with the child reading the text and counting the objects.*

British Library Cataloguing in Publication Data
Murdock, Hy
    One, two, buckle my shoe.
    1. Nursery rhymes in English
    I. Title   II. James, Frank   III. Series
    398'8
    ISBN 0-7214-1265-3

First edition

Published by Ladybird Books Ltd Loughborough Leicestershire UK
Ladybird Books Inc Auburn Maine 04210 USA

© LADYBIRD BOOKS LTD MCMXC

Printed in England

One, two, buckle my shoe

by Hy Murdock
illustrated by Frank James

Ladybird Books

One, two,
buckle my shoe

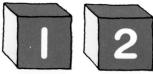

1 2

Count how many...

I have some
new shoes.

*Three, four,
knock at the door*

Count how many...

Here is my house.

Five, six,
pick up sticks

Count how many...

We like to play.

6

Count how many...

I can help.

Count how many...

There are lots of eggs.

6 7 8 9 10

Eleven, twelve,
dig and delve

Count how many...

This is my garden.

Thirteen, fourteen,
maids a-courting

Count how many...

Here are some flowers.

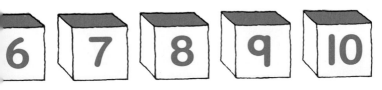

Fifteen, sixteen,
maids in the kitchen

Count how many...

Look at my cake!

6 7 8 9 10

16

Seventeen, eighteen,
maids in waiting

1 2 3 4 5
11 12 13 14 15

Count how many...

Here comes the bus.

6   7   8   9   10

16   17   18

Count how many...

This is my dinner.

Which go together?

3

one

1

three

7

five

9

seven

5

nine

Read these
number words:

one two
three
four five
six seven
eight
nine ten

Do you remember
the rhyme?
Match these pictures
to the words.

Look back in the book
to see if you are right.